LEGO CITY
HALLOWEEN RESCUE!

By Trey King
Illustrated by Sean Wang

SCHOLASTIC INC.

ISBN 978-0-545-51572-6

12 11 10 9 8 7 6 5
Printed in the U.S.A.

14 15 16 17 18/0
40

First printing, July 2013
Designed by Angela Jun

It is Halloween in LEGO® City! The fire department is having a costume party at their new station!

3

There are so many colorful and fun costumes to wear in LEGO City. Even the fire station's Dalmatian is dressed up.

"Bob and Andy! Those are such great costumes. So lifelike!" the chief says, dressed in a gorilla suit. "Could you help get some more ice for the party?"

"Sure," says Andy, dressed as a monster.

"Of course," says Bob, dressed as a werewolf.

Everyone at the party is having so much fun they don't notice a few uninvited guests slipping in the back door.

RING-A-RING-A-RING-A-RING! Suddenly, the fire alarm sounds! Everyone jumps into action.

"Bob, Andy, why are you standing around?" the fire chief asks the Monster and Werewolf. "We've got to go!"

The firefighters put on their fire gear. Then they take their places on the fire truck.

"Quit fooling around!" the chief says to the Monster. "We have a fire to put out!"

"*Mmmmrrrrrr,*" says the Monster.

The firefighters speed off on their truck to put out the fire. They never know what to expect, but they always do their best!

"We're back with more ice!" says the *real* Andy.
"Hey! You can't leave without us!" says the *real* Bob.
"Wait a minute—if we're here, then *who* is on the fire truck in our place?!" asks Andy.

The firefighters arrive at an abandoned house that is on fire. Luckily, no one is in the house.
The team works together quickly to put out the fire.

First they extend the ladder, then they pull out the hose and begin to spray water from above.

On the street, the chief and the Monster hold the hose steady to spray the fire from below.

13

The firemen use an axe and chainsaw to cut through the front door.

Now the other firefighters can go inside and put out the last of the flames with fire extinguishers.

15

The fire chief is proud of his team. "A job well done, everyone," he says.

The Monster helped the fire department put out a fire, but the Werewolf has other things on its mind.

17

"Fire Chief," says a little girl, "can you help get my cat out of that tree?"

"Of course," says the chief.

The fire chief is always prepared—especially for a cat stuck in a tree!

"Look at Bob eat that fish! He knows how to stay in character," the chief jokes.

"Grrrrr!" says the Werewolf.

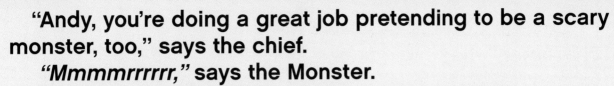

"Andy, you're doing a great job pretending to be a scary monster, too," says the chief.

"*Mmmmrrrrrr,*" says the Monster.

Just then, the *real* Bob and Andy drive up to the scene.

FIRE 60001

"We're so sorry to let you down, sir," Andy says to the fire chief. "We were getting ice when the alarm sounded."
"Who helped you put out the fire?" asks Bob.

"Bob? Andy? I thought *you* were in the monster and werewolf costumes," says the chief.

"Nope," Bob says. "That wasn't us."

The fire chief looks confused. "But if you weren't here, then who helped us?"

The Werewolf and Monster rejoin their friends.
"How was your night?" asks the Vampire.
"Mmmmrrrrrr!" says the Monster.
"Grrrrrr!" says the Werewolf.
"Sounds like the best Halloween ever!" says the Witch.

HAPPY HALLOWEEN

S-TK5-51572-6